Richard Bentley

Patriotism

a mock heroic - in five cantos

Richard Bentley

Patriotism
a mock heroic - in five cantos

ISBN/EAN: 9783337196387

Printed in Europe, USA, Canada, Australia, Japan

Cover: Foto ©Andreas Hilbeck / pixelio.de

More available books at **www.hansebooks.com**

A

MOCK-HEROIC.

IN FIVE CANTOS.

Behold thy Gods, O Israel!

1 KINGS.

LONDON:

Printed for M. HINXMAN, in *Pater-noster-Row.* 1763.
[Price Two Shillings and Six-pence.]

PATRIOTISM,

A

MOCK-HEROIC.

CANTO I.

'TWAS Night; the Voice of Jollity was hush'd,
    Doz'd all her Vot'ries, reasonably flush'd ;
Song, Argument, Invention, Laughter, Jest,
Wit, Bawdry, Criticism, sunk to rest:
Scandal had empty'd all his Tub on BUTE,   5
Abuse of *Royalty* itself was mute.
Sleep in his pleasing Bands had all things ty'd,
All but the Eyes of disappointed PRIDE.

She

She lay revolving in her anxious mind,

How *Refignation* had too much refign'd;   10

That Places were difpens'd as others will'd,

Made vacant fome, and Vacancies were fill'd;

New Statefmen at the Helm ufurp'd her Trade,

And glibly fail'd the Ship without her Aid.

Seeking Repofe from Side to Side fhe flings,   15

No Change of Pofture Paufe of Anguifh brings.

Each grinding Thought Alleviation fcorns,

And fharpens all the Goofe-down into Thorns.

   Forth from the loathed Bed in hafte fhe flew,

And round her weary'd Limbs her Veftments threw. 20

Enwrought with Gold, in Lelac Purple dy'd,

The Velvet cas'd her endlefs Length of Side.

Two calvelefs Bags of Silk then ftretch'd to fee

If they could reach from Heel to diftant Knee.

                                        Next

Next Splay-foot Shoes fhe to her Infteps girt,   25

Shoes which difdain'd, yet ftill were doom'd to Dirt;

Her Thigh fuftain'd a Sword unknown to War,

And beam'd upon her Breaft a Silver Star,

Whofe Rays with magic Influence could warm

Almoft to Confequence the languid Form.   30

Accoutred thus, forth of her Doors fhe went,

And her dark Vifit was to FACTION bent;

Refolv'd, like Heav'n-rejeated *Saul*, to try

What Counfel t'other Party might fupply.

Onward fhe ftrides, impatient of Delay,   35

Flound'ring thro' ev'ry Kennel in her Way;

Save that at *Charing-crofs* fhe flack'd her Tread,

And thought fhe faw poor *Charles* without his Head.

Re-haft'ning on thro' the long *Strand* fhe came,

Then pafs'd the *Temple*, and ador'd its Name;   40

Now

Now reach'd St. *Paul's*, and blefs'd the Lord that there
Tho' He was prais'd, 'twas with unwilling Pray'r.
Next in a grateful Rapture ftretch'd to *Bow*,
And heard th' *unmuffled* Tongue of Night ftrike Two.
Acknowledging the Omen, fhe advanc'd,   45
While fudden Vigour thro' each Sinew danc'd.

High on a hundred Columns, whofe dead Weight
Preffes the ruftic Bafe in aukward State,
Where hardly they fuftain, their Shafts unbent,
The Load of Cornice, and of Pediment   50
Which rough with Sculpture in ftrong Emblem clad,
Tells us, That Riches make a City mad;
The pond'rous Manfion-houfe of Faction ftands,
Rais'd by o'er-reaching Heads and griping Hands.

                                        Before

Before the Gate, a Giant fierce and fell,   55
Stalk'd *Oppofition*, dreadful Centinel !
And *Who goes there*, he cry'd, *yourfelf explain* ;
A Friend, fhe faid, *to Denmark*, *not the Dane*.
Her well-known Voice he recollected ftrait,
Quick every Bolt fhoots backward on the Gate,   60
Bolts to endure which never own'd the Pow'r,
But only made to ferve the prefent Hour,
And yet the very beft, for Strength and Size,
The Blackfmith's *Place* and *Penfion* could devife.

Of canker'd Brafs and rufty Ir'n each Door,   65
Stood maffive, fpirtled thick with human Gore,
Which Popularity for ever draws
From Fools, in Patriot-Rebellion's Caufe.
Open they burft, with defperate Recoil,
The jarring Hinges fcream for want of Oil,   70

Loud

Loud and difcordant, as when Civil Rage

Incites two kindred Armies to engage.

Near *Aylefbury* firft caught the horrid Sound,

And echo'd all its Terrors with rebound,

Concord at diftant *Stowe* perceiv'd the Yell,   75

While down her ill-adapted Vizor fell;

Extremeft *Exeter* rock'd to the Noife,

And aided its hoarfe Thunder with her Voice:

At once her Cyders four, and all around

Her Apple-bloffoms ftrew the blufhing Ground.   80

And now, where yawn'd the Portal rude and vaft,

To Faction's Refidence the Goddefs paft.

Clofe to the Door, in the firft Veftibule,

Sat *Clamour, Riot, Infult,* and *Mifrule,*

Stern *Menace, Licence* grown to dang'rous fize,   85

Reproach, and an Infinitude of *Lyes.*

A thoufand

A thoufand Voices bellow through the Room,

A thoufand Echoes clatter 'gainft the Dome ;

Copious, but unconnected Eloquence,

Words of fierce Import, but of little Senfe ;   90

Not meant to mean, and therefore to appear

More irritative to the vulgar Ear.

There might be heard, 'midft other piercing Cries,

Liberty ! Property ! and no Excife !

Of *Magna Charta* the more dreadful Roar ;   95

Prerogative, and arbitrary Pow'r--- :

There *Habeas-corpus* howl'd, from Jail broke loofe,

Slav'ry, and Privilege, and wooden Shoes---

Corruption, Favourites, and no Addrefs---

And uncontroul'd the Licence of the Prefs :   100

Sounds that all Senfe of Order could erafe,

But get the Man, who breaks thro' all, a Place.

B

Stun'd

Stun'd with the deaf'ning Peal fhe pafs'd along,

(Yet paffing would carefs the friendly Throng)

Thro' vaft Saloons which fpoke *May'r-royal* State, 105

Rich without Tafte, and without Grandeur, great.

Yet here the Chiffel and the Pencil ftrove

Beft to record the Objects of Mob-love.

Tribunes, and Ephori, and Demagogues,

By Men call'd Patriots, but by Gods plain Rogues; 110

Such as, provided they themfelves grew great,

Had no Objection to fubvert a State.

Nor wanted here each dirty, dreadful Job,

That *Faction* perpetrates to pleafe the Mob.

To pleafe the Mob, here mighty *Strafford* bled,   115

And *Laud* laid down his venerable head.

To pleafe the Mob, *Byng* ftains the blufhing Deep,

And *Blakeney* earns a Peerage in his Sleep.

                                        To

To pleafe the Mob, our Fleets their Canvas ftrain,

And Expeditions hide the wond'ring Main,   120

The Main more wond'ring wafts us back, alas !

Thin'd from the Wars of *Rochfort* and *St. Cas :*

What matter ? fince Defeat our Joy infpires,

And *Caffel* loft can light a thoufand Fires.

By having pleas'd the Mob, here *Cromwell* ftood, 125

And fhew'd how private thrives by public Good ;

And might have fhewn us Gulls, if Gulls could fee,

That *Slav'ry* tracks th' Abufe of *Liberty.*

Confefs'd at length the Patriot-Tyrant reign'd,

And fnapt that Freedom *Charles* had only ftrain'd. 130

Hampden was here, in his *Eidolon* here,

A would-be Tutor to the Royal Heir,

But he himfelf dwells in the Fields of Fame,

Wedded to Liberty's immortal Name.

And here in Tints more recent might be view'd, 135

Inftructive Picture of Court Gratitude !

How round their Sov'reign his great Servants ftand,

While fierce *Rebellion* gores the bleeding Land;

Faith, Honour, Duty, Loyalty, the Laws,

Urge them, no doubt, to perifh in his Caufe ?   140

No, but to ferve with *Granville* they refufe;

So great a Crime in Monarchs 'tis, to *chufe!*

A hundred other equal Deeds appear,

Nay, half the *Englifh* Hiftory was here.

While, over all the reft, confpicuous fhines   145

Old *Sarah*'s Legacy in Golden Lines.

Around in lefs Compartments were beftow'd

Of underling Incendiaries a Crowd,

Such as employ'd the Pulpit or the Prefs,

T' enforce the Doctrines of Licentioufnefs ;   150

Here

Here *Party* canoniz'd fuch Denizens,
Whofe Ears had paid the Forfeit of their Pens;
And while in all her glaring Daub fhe paints,
Villains grow Heroes, Scoundrels turn to Saints.

Our Goddefs midft the reft herfelf defcry'd,   155
Mix'd with the Leaders of the *other Side*;
" And, ah! fhe faid, the very Walls can trace,
" How often we change Principles for Place."

END of CANTO I.

P A-

PATRIOTISM,

A

MOCK-HEROIC.

CANTO II.

IN the Recess of something like a Tomb,
   Which *Architecture*, (sick of *Greece* and *Rome*,
And copying what never was at all,)
Is pleas'd to christen an *Egyptian Hall*;
Our Goddess, whom She sought, at length survey'd, 5
In anti-kingly Majesty array'd.
Busy she found Him in this solemn place,
At solemn Sacrifice, with solemn Face.

He

He but to *Commerce* fcorn'd to pour a Pray'r;
No other Deity employ'd his Care;   10
All other Altars ftood inconfecrate;
For her's no Offering was too pure or great.

Of folid Gold, and of enormous fize;
Yet not fo big her Belly as her Eyes,
She ftood; and feem'd as fhe would hide the Globe   15
Beneath the Drap'ry of her flowing Robe.
Faft by, with full Extent of Gullet grac'd,
Her Attribute, the *Cormorant*, was plac'd.

The Victims He had taken Care to cull,
All without Blemifh, all of blackeft Wool,   20
All newly bought, all newly flay'd alive,
A Decatomb, of Negro Slaves twice five.

He on their reeking Mufcles, red and blue,

Sharp Vinegar, with Salt and Pepper, threw;

They writh with Pain convolv'd. As when to cram   25

Some Citizen's unfathomable Wem,

The Turtle, riven with his Mail, poor Fifh!

Perceives himfelf begin to grow a Difh;

Convuls'd, each undulating Fibre plays

In Waves of Agony a thoufand ways.   30

So fixt the inextinguifhable Soul,

That drefs'd, perhaps he feels thy teeth, K * *.

    The Goddefs, no Confufion to create,

Impatient as fhe was, thought fit to wait:

Civilities are ne'er fo duly paid   35

To any Folks, as when we want their Aid.

The Ceremony, with Obfervance meek

She 'tended, and when done, began to fpeak.

                        " Oh

" O Thou ! for whom and from whom I was form'd,

" Whofe Counfel moulded, and whofe Spirit warm'd, 40

" To whom originally 'tis I owe

" Thefe purple Honours, which around me glow,

" To Thee I come my Sorrows to impart ;

" Reft fhuns thefe Eyes, and Care corrodes this Heart :

" Do thou affift, in this Conjunction nice, 45

" Me and the Party with thy fage Advice.

" Thus far, indeed, Succefs has crown'd our Arms,

" BUTE quits; nor fhaken with our fierce Alarms,

" For who our Roar and Riot would regard,

" That in his Confcience feeks for his Reward ? 50

" But that the honeft Fool had fix'd before

" To make his fav'rite Peace, and throw up Pow'r.

" When he like *Phineas* in the Gap had ftood,

" To fave the People, and had ftaunch'd their Blood,

C " He

" He knew how incompatible muſt prove,　　　55

" To ſerve them, yet retain their fickle Love.

" While we play'd ſafe, Dupe of Benevolence!

" He ſtop'd the Plague, and at his own Expence,

" For public Quiet, yielding up that Rein

" We quitted, only to reſume again.　　　60

" But what are we the better than before?

" Our empty Niches know us all no more;

" Still the State Truncheon flys our eager Graſp,

" And Calumny is at its lateſt Gaſp.

" What to do next! Inſult can do no more,　　65

" Higher than *Forty-five* it cannot ſoar,

" Where, to full Pitch of ſturdy Vigour grown,

" It fairly gives the Lye home to the T----e:

" Nothing remains which farther we can drive,

" Or *Forty-eight* comes next to *Forty-five*.　　70

　　　　　　　　　　　　　　" Then

" Then fhall we idly fit, hand-cuff'd and dumb,

" And let Truth work, and purge away the Scum

" We have fermented ? let the Drofs dejeɛ̃,

" Till its clear Bofom fhall all Heav'n reflect ?

" Forbid it Fate! forbid it ev'ry Boaft   75

" We've made to ruin,. or to rule the Roaft!

" We muft and will have All ; but how to feize,

" To fpill the Cyder, or cut down the Trees,

" More Suits at Law commence, more Papers write,

" To give more Dinners, and more Guefts invite,   80

" Or the deep, fatal Train to touch with Flame,

" And fire all *Aylefbury* and *Buckingham*,

" I come to afk ; thy Counfel be my Guide."

She faid, and FACTION to her thus reply'd.

" To raife the Mob by Mafter-Strokes of Art,   85

" Inflame the Paffions, and miflead the Heart,

" Make happy Subjects furfeit on their Eafe,

" Repine at Bleffings, and grow fick of Peace,----

" To pour the Multitude which way we lift,

" And ere they're injur'd, fet them to refift,   90

" Halloo them on, to roar with frantic Zeal,

" Againft Oppreffions which no Soul can feel,

" Till they defire to fpill their defp'rate Lives,

" For Printers' 'Prentices' Prerogatives ;----

" To bid a little River flow along   95

" The fole Criterion to know Right from Wrong,

" With ev'ry Lafh of Infamy impel

" The farther Side, becaufe it *won't* rebel,----

" On all who dare imply we do amifs,

" Point ready Obloquy's infulting Hifs;   100

" Hold

" Hold up, in whomfoe'er we difapprove,

" (And that means all who fhare their Mafter's Love)

" Virtue or Genius, like th' Athenian Owl,

" To the blunt Peck of ev'ry other Fowl;

" All the Humanity of BUTE to blot,   105

" And all thy Candour, MANSFIELD, fink in *Scot*;---

" Recaft the Royal Virtues, which before

" The Nation worfhipp'd, and cry down the Ore,

" To teach the People this indulgent Reign,

" With ev'ry Charge of Tyranny to ftain,   110

" To fwallow any Contradiction down,

" In *Antonine*'s mild Look fear *Nero*'s Frown,

" Wreft his Intention, and diftort each Fact,

" And lend them Treafon till they long to act---

" The Prince againft his Counfellors to move,   115

" And while we only feem to beg, reprove,

                                        " In

" In Terms of Duty wrap each boiſt'rous Deed,

" Kneel while we ſtab, and libel while we plead,

" FACTION has Pow'r; nay, has already done,

" And yet but little of our Courſe we've run,   120

" Much ſtill remains; and we muſt tug and ſtrive

" Ere the great Days of Anarchy revive:

" A watchful Eye is over all our Game,

" And while it ſeems to wink, but takes its Aim.

" Oh! had but Fate to HALIFAX decreed   125

" His Seat of Birth on t'other Side the *Tweed*!

" Had ſome bleak Shire, of Penury the Reign,

" More ſtarv'd than *Famine's Prophecy* can feign,

" But giv'n him Title, in the gen'ral Ban,

" We with the Country, had o'erwhelm'd the Man; 130

" There like *Enceladus* he'd lain oppreſs'd,

" With half an Iſland bearing on his Breaſt.

But

" But now, upon fo high a Bafis plac'd,

" We're forc'd to leave his Merit undefac'd;

" Out of our Reach, and mocking of our Aim,   135

" The perfeƐt Statue refts without a Maim.

" But could we hope his Virtues to decry,

" And fhew them blighted to the People's Eye;

" Would not *Ïerne* all their Bloom renew,

" And call the blufhing Honours frefh in View?   140

" Recount, how Lenity to Prudence join'd

" Shone the Reflexion of his Sender's Mind;

" How form'd to win by ev'ry honeft Art,

" Blefs'd by each Voice, and Lord of ev'ry Heart;

" Yet, when a Nation prefs'd him to receive   145

" All that a Nation's Gratitude could give,

" The ftrong Allure of Int'reft he withftood,

" Above Reward, and paid by, doing good?

" Here

" Here then we ftick; but ftill of Hope a Gleam

" Points thro' the dufky Thought its trembling Beam, 150

" The Deities, from Heav'n felf-exil'd, meet

" At a grand Council, and a grander Treat,

" To-morrow.   Such AMBITION's high Beheft,

" And FOLLY does the Honours of the Feaft.

" Be there, the beft Advice fure to receive,   155

" If Multitude of Counfellors can give :

" Till then beneath this Roof remain my Gueft,

" 'Tis Break of Day, and Time to go to reft.

So faying, her Attendants fhe bid fpread

For her great Vifitant the lofty Bed.   160

And firft the Fox's Skin began the Pile,

Next of the Bear was fpread the fhaggy Spoil,

And

And over that the Lion's tawny Hide
Finiſh'd the whole for diſappointed Pride.
There ev'ry Pore, as ſhe extended laid,
Imbib'd Inſtruction from the myſtic Bed.

END of CANTO II.

P A-

P A T R I O T I S M,

A

M O C K - H E R O I C.

C A N T O III.

OH for the warning Voice of Him who faw
    What Ruin continental Meafures draw,
What Time by perjurable *Styx* he fwore
To wafte on them nor Man nor Guinea more;
That yet the People, made in Time aware,   5
Might haply 'fcape *Sedition*'s dang'rous Snare!

For now the rolling Hours brought on, too foon!
The Day, whofe Morn as ufual rofe at Noon,

I

Wherein

Wherein th' Arch-Enemy to Peace began

To meet in deep Confult her dark Divan :   10

The Sun conceal'd in Fogs his fullen Ray,

And dreadful Omens ufher'd in the Day.

Forth from his *G---ge-S---t* Airy upwards fprings

The fierce *North-Briton* on audacious Wings ;

Th' encumber'd Air could fcarce fuftain this Fowl,   15

Which dares an Eagle, tho' it *looks an Owl.

Undazzled he beholds the tow'ring Height,

And to Olympus lifts his defp'rate Flight.

Next him uprofe, and of as bad Portent,

On Wings, ah Pity ! by the Mufes lent,   20

A Black-bird erft in fober Liv'ry dreft,

Now Party-colour'd Plumage ftains his Breaft ;

D 2

Paffion

* See HOGARTH.

Paſſion had chang'd his old Appearance meek,

And arm'd his Talons, and hook'd down his Beak :

His Pinion ſtrong, if Dirt depreſs'd it not,   25

And ſweet his Throat would it cry aught but *Scot*---

Neglected ſoon we let the Parrot roar,

Whoſe Dictionary knows but Rogue and Whore.

Of lower Flight, ſcarce hov'ring from the Ground,

The *Monitor* his leſſer Circle wound ;   30

The Vultur he, of old whom *Jove* ſevere,

(That *Jove* who would direct this nether Sphere,)

Ordain'd thro' *H---d*'s Sides to bore his Way,

And on his growing Vitals weekly prey.

And theſe behind, with boding, croaking Cry,   35

The *Contraſt* ſeem'd to flutter, not to fly.

While

While hopp'd on either Side, pert, noify, light, ·
The Magpye *Gazetteer*, half black, half white.

Around, on ev'ry Part, whole Flocks arofe
Of Rooks and Ravens, Chronicles and Crows ;   40
Fann'd by innumerable Pens, the Sky
Of Printer's Ink affum'd the fable Dye.

Now prone from his Meridian, when the Sun
Had more than half his Evening Journey run,
And FOLLY's Board, loaded almoft to break,   45
Had well nigh cool'd her fav'ry Steam ; to fpeak
Thrice PRIDE effay'd; but from her Elbow Chair
As oft AMBITION nodded to forbear :
She ftopp'd, fo wont t' obey.   And now each Gueft
Perceiv'd that Nature wanted to digeft.   50

Juft

Juſt then a hundred Servants croud the Space,

Who ne'er ſaw Wages but in Shape of Place,

And up they pile the vaſt Deſert in Air;

(The Plate of Gold by Rule of Court was there)

Where *Robinſon* had play'd his Maſter Part,   55

And in one Job exhauſted all the Art.

High in the midſt of the whole Fabric rais'd,

A Barley-ſugar Miniſter was plac'd,

His Comfit Promiſes who round him throws

On Dreſden-China Courtiers rang'd in Rows.   60

So juſt the Artiſt did his Skill diſplay,

Ev'n in the Gift they ſeem'd to melt away.

Cloſe at his Side, and wond'ring ſhe was ſweet,

Juſtice no longer ſtern, poſſeſs'd her Seat :

The

The Mafter had her Likenefs hit fo pat, . . 65
You'd fwear fhe was the Sifter of J---e P---t.

Beneath in Sugar, as in Crime, combin'd,
Were HALIFAX and EGREMONT defign'd:.
The noble Robbers ftood in flagrant Act,
A ftol'n Brafs Candleftick confefs'd the Fact. 70

And oppofite in *Naples* Bifcuit rofe,
Whofe Moat in Green and Silver Tiffue flows,
The guilty Tow'r of *Julius*; all around
In Orange-peel its dreadful Warders frown'd,
And feem'd to tread, Sight horrid and unmeet! 75
A Wafer MAGNA-CHARTA under Feet.

There round a Chariot, thro' the parted Throng,
In Bronze the threat'ning Bruifers march'd along;

The

The decent Mob, fuch Fear within them dwelt,

Retire to Diſtance, and forbear to pelt.   80

   Here, in the Front, was form'd a ſumptuous Feaſt,

And ſeem'd both great and amiable the Gueſt;

Giv'n to whoſe Name the outward Form appear'd,

But the ſly Honours at another leer'd.   84

Th' immenſe Pile ſtood compleat; the whole to ſhape,

Quite round the ruddy Apple mourn'd in Crape.

All prais'd the Hand, and the Deſign admir'd,

Warm'd as they gaz'd, but when they taſted, fir'd.

   Now *Loyalty* begins the ſacred Health,

On which *Sedition* only creeps by Stealth: 90

The Toaſts, ſtill as they wander from their Source,

Shew more evanid its diluted Force.

                       As

As when, all-graceful MARLBOROUGH, your Dress

Tell us that *Ranelagh* you mean to bless,   95

While down your perfect Form in Rainbow Rows,

The Luteſtring Stripe with gay Confuſion flows;

The Point infenſible, (the Diff'rence ſeen)

Where Purple ſteals to Yellow, or to Green:

We find, deluded thro' the varying Silks,   99

That what commenc'd with G--- concludes with W---

I truſt that Heav'n the *Thracian* did deſtroy,

Pervertor firſt of Toaſting, born to Joy,

Who mingled Int'reſt with the Flow of Soul,

And daſh'd with Party, Friendſhip's ſmiling Bowl.

Menace and fell Revenge lurk to be quaff'd   105

In the foul Bottom of the dang'rous Draught.

              E   At

At FOLLY's Board no Mifchief ftalk'd behind,

For People out of Place are of one Mind,

Jointly they hunt; but Diff'rence and Debate

Come when they fhare the Bear's-fkin of the State.   110

. And now in general Difcourfe they join,

So tipfy with the Healths, not with the Wine,

That Cuftom, Reafon, Fact, are chang'd and chopp'd,

To all that Modern Patriots adopt.

All fpoke, and all advis'd a thoufand Things,   115

To buoy up Citizens and weigh down Kings;

And fome direct the Matter how to mince,

And mean by evil Counfellors, the Prince,

How turn Militia to a Counter-Guard,

And while difbanded Valour they reward,   120

(Humanity can never be a Crime,)

They keep it ready till a proper Time.

Some

Some mourn the Injuries They groan beneath,

Who owe to Courts the very Air they breathe,

Who, one fmall Boon deny'd, thofe Courts refift, 125

And but for that, that only, are difmifs'd:

As to paft Favours---ftaunch State-Atheifts fay,

Duty, the Soul, dies with its Body, Pay.

Some tell the ready way on Mobs t' impofe,

Whofe Sight extends no farther than their Nofe. 130

To whom Conviction never found its Way,

They ftill believe the P-----y of the Day.

Others advance how Squabbles make us great,

And cutting Throats adds Sinews to a State.

What Profits burgeon from domeftic Jars, 135

And all the Bleffings fhow'r'd on Civil Wars:

The Song was partial, yet it took the Ear

Of all who fought their Thoufand Pounds a Year.

 When

When FOLLY, to give Order to Debate,

Stood up a mighty Driveller of State,   140

Ridiculoufly grand, her Cap and Bells

Important Infignificance conceals.

A Petticoated *Neftor* fhe appears,

Bending beneath unvenerable Years.

A fhrivell'd Evidence how very fmall   145

A Share of Reafon goes to rule this Ball;

Two Reigns fhe'd blunder'd thro' ftill uppermoft,

Quitted the third, nor gave the fourth for loft.

With Manna ftill her Tongue run o'er replete,

Thick, clammy, mawkifh, purgatively fweet,   150

And fell her Words like Hail in Summer Day,

As hard, as cold, as apt to melt away.

The *Lingua-Franca* Sediment of School

Where She mifs'd Science mark'd her ftill more Fool;

Which, with fix Latin Shreds, conn'd o'er with Pain, 155

Wove the loofe Texture of her flimfy Brain.

Now her No-meaning to exprefs fhe ftrives,

With all that Confidence which Nonfenfe gives.

" My Voice fhall be for open War, oh Peers !

" It fuits fo well my Temper and my Years. 160

" Which unimpair'd preferve their wonted Fire,

" Demand Employ, and fcorn the Word RETIRE ;

" Nor from my Shoulders think their Burthen great,

" Years do not prefs from Number but from Weight.

" Oh were I but as young, high in Renown, 165

" As when one H---r apparent to the C---n,

" I at a royal Chrift'ning dar'd provoke,

" Deferv'd his Menace, tho' I 'fcap'd its Stroke ;

" Or when, tho' fomewhat doubled then with Age,

" The next to him I glory'd to engage ! 170

" Witnefs ye Banks of *Cam*, that overthrow,

" When thy dull Stream had Doubts which Way to flow,

" 'Till

" 'Till I triumphant won the laurell'd Day,

" And the difputed Title bore away!

" Forgive the Boafts, Me, fince they ferve to fhew, 175

" To Infult, nor to Oppofition new.

" That glorious Monarch, (fo we call Him now,

" Whom when alive we treated God knows how,

" Whom ev'n the *City* now reveres, yet then

" Would not fo much as hear of *Dettinghen*)   180

" Saw, when his Scepter trembled in his Hand,

" Me foremoft in the Files of Quitters ftand.

" Nor think I fingle lift in your Defign,

" The Men who laugh at me, for me refign,

" Themfelves from what they have in Hand feclude, 185

" While Hope of more appears like Gratitude;

                                        " Thefe

" Thefe all increafe your Bands with ready Aid,

" Forces the Court againft itfelf has paid.

" Lead on, I follow, glad to have arraign'd,

" Whatever Meafures my whole Life maintain'd :   190

" Convictive Contradictions come about,

" Seen in the different Lights of *in* and *out*.

" Did I its general Extent allow ?

" I fee th' Excife in all its Horrors now.

" Againft the *Craftfman* did my Writ prevail,   195

" And fend poor *Franklyn* o'er and o'er to Jail ?

" Now, perifh'd Liberty ! I mourn aloud,

" Thy Fall by Forms, which then the Law avow'd !

" Made I, of Heads like mine with Numbers more,

" Such War and Peace as ne'er were made before ?   200

2   The

" The prefent Peace with Energy I hate,

" And kneel before the Word INADEQUATE.

" Or was my Judgment formerly inclin'd,

" To think Addreffes fpoke the People's Mind?

" Inftructed, now I fee their full Import,   205

" Againft they do, but never for, a Court:

" And yet it hurts me that It is addrefs'd,

" But when by *Cambridge*, more than all the reft"----

Th' o'erwhelming Thought fhe could no longer bear,
But fputt'ring ftill to fpeak, funk to her Chair.

E N D of C A N T O III.

P A-

PATRIOTISM,

A

MOCK-HEROIC.

CANTO IV.

IN ftudy'd Dignity of Action flow,
 Befpeaking Favour with a winning Bow,
AMBITION next arofe. Her pow'rful Lore,
Credulity preventive ftepp'd before:
For *Eloquence*, the Cheat, had brought her up 5
To all the Slight-hand of the Ball and Cup;
Taught her to twift, and turn, and fhew, and hide,
And make the worfe appear the better Side;

F Shew'd

Shew'd her, to clafh how Contradictions ceas'd,
While Fact and Reafon took what Shape fhe pleas'd. 10

As the bright Stream, which Nature loves to pour
Irriguous thro' the Vale, had nurs'd each Flow'r,
Had charm'd the Ear and Eye thro' op'ning Glades,
With untaught Murmurs from unforc'd Cafcades;
But when comprefs'd thro' Pipes, as Whim prevails, 15
Squirts into Fans, and Suns, and Peacocks Tails:
The glitt'ring Baubles who with Wonder fpies,
Receives the Spout at laft in his own Eyes.

And thus fhe faid: " O Thou, who doft prefide
" O'er *Britain's* Ifle, and all her Meafures guide,   20
" Whofe Doctrine Heav'n's own Precept far out-goes,
" Bids us love, better than ourfelves, our Foes;

Of

" O *Janus-Party!* now incline to hear

" Thy double Face and thy quadruple Ear.

" And ye, now prefent, to my Nod devote,   25

" Lords, and Lords Betters, Aldermen ! take note

" That FOLLY to my Bofom here I bend,

" Her, my Contempt till now, but now my Friend :

" Link'd in the common Caufe fhe fhall remain

" My firm Confed'rate, till I rule again.   30

" 'Twere needlefs here to tell, what yet you fee

" Draws its conceal'd, dim, Origin from me---

" The Rage of Faction, when each Nerve it moves,

" He who does not difclaim, be fure approves.

" Behold! the Cloud, I faid, would threat the Land, 35

" That Cloud fhall rife in Likenefs of this Hand,

" Pour all its Storms, directed as I pleafe,

" And wafh away the hateful Works of Peace :

F 2

Works

" Works, which myfelf I dar'd not bring about,

" I knew them right, but knew they'd throw me out.

" Another ventur'd, foolifh, or fecure   41

" In his own Soul, and above Luft of Pow'r,

" Seal'd the great Deed to which his Wifh afpir'd,

" And unrewarded, but by That, retir'd.

" And could he think, of Peace the Foe profeft   45

" Title and Penfion had inclin'd to Reft ?

" That on AMBITION's Eye Repofe would creep,

" Lull'd by thofe medicated Sops to fleep ?

" She who twin'd Unanimity, and fhew'd

" The wond'ring World how firm *Britannia* ftood,   50

" Can the reverted Wheel as quick incite,

" Till all the fplitting Fibres difunite.

" She

" She who fell Party's tortuous Folds could break,

" And fet her Foot upon that Dragon's Neck, 54

" The deadly Teeth, which from thofe Jaws fhe drew,

" Can plant, and they can pullulate anew.

" Thofe Grains of Difcord giv'n to fertile Land

" Sprout rank, and faithful to the Sower's Hand.

" Yes, in ripe Harveft fee them nod again,

" A threatning Crop of difcontented Men; 60

" Which Way to wave they from my Breath expect,

" Blame as I point, and hate as I direct.

" It grieves me FOLLY, nay it gives me Fears,---

" This foul Defection of your black Huffars,

" Whofe wav'ring Duty, truant from its String, 65

" Transfers itfelf from C-----r to K---g.

" Now by the Laurels of *Belleifle*, my Boaft,

" And the unnumber'd Millions which they coft,

" Should

" Shoul'd e'er my B----h for addreſſing move,

" And honeſt A---n dare the Peace approve,   70

" In ſuch Contempt the Rebels I ſhould hold,

" I'd toſs them back their dirty Box of Gold !

    " But ere th' Infection ſpreads, haſte we to uſe

" The Sp'rit we've been ſo happy to infuſe;

" The *Engliſh Oak-boy* as you bid him crys,   75

" And to roar louder firmly ſhuts his Eyes:

" He's yours at Pleaſure clos'd while they remain,

" All's over if he opens them again.

" Employ him while, all Enemies o'ercome,

" He longs for new ones in his Friends at home,   80

" The proper Catch-words *Party* ſhall provide,

" To range the Fools on either fooliſh Side;

" No previous Injury need rouſe their Force,

" Match but the *Broughtons,* and they hate of Courſe.

" Oh, if we feize with Skill the coming Hour, 85

" And re-inveft us with the Robe of Pow'r,

" Rule while we live! Let future Days tranfmute

" To ev'ry Merit all we've charg'd on BUTE ;

" Let late Pofterity receive his Name,

" And fwell its Sails with ev'ry Breath of Fame ;

" Downward, as far as Time fhall roll his Tide, 90

" With ev'ry Pennant flying, let it glide,

" And Truth, emerging from the Clouds we raife,

" Gild all their Orient Colours with her Blaze.

" Let his lov'd Arts, attendant on his Way, 95

" Their wanton Trophies to the Gale difplay ;

" While each difpaffionate, each honeft Pen

" (Deterr'd by Clamour, nor allur'd by Gain,

" Bard or Hiftorian) fhall from either Shore 99

" Hail its Approach, and its great Courfe explore ;

" Faithful

" Faithful to Probity, and Virtue's Caufe,

" Purfue its Progrefs, and direct th' Applaufe :

" Glad Gratulation fhall with Shouts approve,

" And own him worthy of his Sov'reign's Love."

She had proceeded, but the mingled Sound   105

Of arguing Voices fpread the Table round,

Some affirm'd pofitive, fome afk'd perplext,

And fome launch'd out in Notes upon the Text ;

Till one more audible than all the reft,

With ftrong Exertion thus himfelf exprefs'd :   110

" Why fit we here projecting fome new Blow,

" Since FATE determins all Events below ?

" On that Tribunal let our Envoy wait,

" And who fo fit as FOLLY upon FATE ? "

Th'

Th' Advice was grateful to the gen'ral Ear,   1 1 5
All beg'd that great Commiſſion ſhe would bear,
Which, bowing low, ſhe ſaid ſhould be atchiev'd,
Tho' trembling at the Honour ſhe receiv'd ;
The Point thus ſettled, from the Board they move,
Diſpers'd as Pleaſure led, or Bus'neſs drove.   1 2 0

But FOLLY ſought her Library with Speed,
For one ſhe had for Show, but not to read,
There jumbling in her Head what ſhe thought, Thought,
How beſt to find the trackleſs Road ſhe ſought,
She choſe t'eſſay the Force of her own Prate,   1 2 5
Remembring to how many once 'twas Fate.

And now the myſtic Gibberiſh ſhe tried,
Something that neither promis'd nor deny'd,

G

But

But drew one on to hope, " it wifh'd fo well ---

" And though it doubted, yet---it could not tell--- 130

" O! my dear *What's-your-Name*, of me be fure,

" I would a Member had not afk'd before---

" You'll let me fee you foon, by then I'll try"---

Then feem'd to fqueeze a Hand, and faid, Good-by.

Strange Force of Charms ! By this the folid Ground

Grew mortal fick with the unmeaning Sound,   136

In ftrong Convulfions rock'd ; at length it cleft,

And a wide Opening tow'rds the Center left,

To Regions unexplor'd, which, dark and great,

Are the Domain of MYSTERY-OF-STATE.   140

Pond'ring a while fhe ftood, and wifh'd to know

The *Calais*-Paffage to thefe Realms below,

'Till Curiofity her Fears expung'd,

And fhe intrepid on her Errand plung'd.

Now, as she journey'd, faded on her Sight   145
The feeble Glimmerings of distant Light,
Faint and more faint the intercepted Ray
Withdrew itself, and died upon her Way.
And now, thro' Darkness, palpable, abhorr'd,
Her groping Hands the doubtful Path explor'd,   150
'Till nigh the Confines, where the lower Sphere
Joins to our World, but yet is ne'er the near,
Thin Streaks of budding Day salute her Eye
With the first Dawnings of the nether Sky;
For other Suns they have and Stars than we,   155
By which no Mortal but themselves can see.

Now the receding Gloom her Sight renew'd,
And cloath'd with Form each bright'ning Object stood.
The opening Scene with Wonder she surveys,
Not knowing that she travell'd her own Ways,   160

G 2   Here

Here for the upper Surface fhe difcern'd,

How Flatt'ry lay to bubling Lather churn'd,

Whofe Bottom form'd a thicker Sediment

Of coarfe and clumfy Clergy Compliment.

This happy Compoft with its fupple Oil   165

Invigorates and opes the fertile Soil,

Calls forth each Seed of Dirt to bud and flow'r,

And trick itfelf in all the Hues of Pow'r;

While from her Urn Partiality fupplies

The Stream, to Blood and Merit, fhe denies.   170

Hence blooms th' unlearn'd Divine in all the Glow

His double-petall'd Mitre can beftow,

Hence fpreads the Under Clerk his ample fhoot,

And ftrikes in the Revenue deep his Root,

Hence high his flourifh'd Head the Valet rears,   185

And hence Attornies bloffom into Peers.

Still

Still lower, in their different Strata fpread,

As Levity thought fit to range, were laid

Clofe in their Shells involv'd, yet innocent,

The unhatch'd Vermin of a Government.   180

Here Grubs and Maggots Favour's Sun-fhine wait,

To get new Shapes, and wing the World in State,

Or more induftrious, fnug, and warm as Milk,

Spin their foft Nefts, and wrap themfelves in Silk.

Here Snails of Office thro' their flimy Tracks   185

Crawl off at laft with Houfes on their Backs.

Hence Worms and Earwigs in new Figures fport,

And tinge themfelves in ev'ry Dye of Court,

'Till pinch'd with Cold, another Form they try,

And dip their varying Films in LIBERTY.   190

Here yet unfang'd, wriggle the Viper Race,

Which fond Adminiftration broods in Place,

'Till

'Till fatten'd on herſelf, and fit for Strife,

They thro' her Bowels gnaw their way to Life.

Here public Zeal, the Alligator, hides   195

Her ſelfiſh Eggs, and for their Birth provides,

Of Incubation in no Need they ſtand,

But hatch in Popularity's hot Sand;

To prey with open Mouths away they ſcour,

Yet ſeem to mourn the Country they devour.   200

Now lower as ſhe went the hoary Deep

Diſcovers where the Seeds of Metals ſleep.

She ſaw, and lik'd to ſee, the plodding Head

Do the World's Buſ'neſs, yet be only Lead;

That Impudence, its Copper Birth forgot,   205

Grows Braſs, and is important on the Spot;

That Talk and Pertneſs ſtill ſucceed by Din,

And ſhine and tinkle in the Shape of Tin;

That

That Ignorance and Meannefs rais'd to Pow'r,

Their low Materials quickly filver o'er ;   210

That Whig and Tory Principles unfold

Their like Conftituence, and turn to Gold.

But Wit, the Quick-filver, efcap'd her View,

Or feeing what it was fhe little knew,

Laft faw, where Party-Gems their Rays refine,   215

How Patriotifm inflames the blazing Mine.

She now perceiv'd, from this inftructive Sight,

A kind of Reminifcence, all was right.

The Soul is never taught, but recollects   220

The Traces of its prior Intellects,

Acknowleges the State fhe held before,

And owns the beaming Shield at Troy fhe bore.

PATRIOTISM,

A

MOCK-HEROIC.

CANTO V.

OF perfect Diamond a folid Rock,
  Far from the Tempeſt's Beat and Earthquake's Shock,
Its maſſive Spurs down to the Center ſhoots,
Where endleſs Permanency binds the Roots;
Upon its Summit awefully elate   5
Immoveably is fix'd the Throne of FATE:
The wond'rous Pile no Mark of Structure ſhews,
Unhewn, unbuilt, the living Quarry grows.

Up

Up the fteep Height an Iron Caufeway tends,
And at the Footftool of the Monarch ends ;   10
Here FOLLY pafs'd, and as fhe climb'd the Mound,
Hollow and loud her fhuffling Steps refound.

Rais'd on his Seat the hoary Sire appear'd,
And fpread profufe his ample Flow of Beard ;
No Condefcenfion his firm Looks avow,   15
Inexorable Sternnefs knits his Brow.
Around him bawl, but clam'rous to no End,
The fond Addreffes which we Mortals fend ;
He to their Purport turns a deafen'd Ear,
Or anfwers traverfly the wafted Pray'r ;   20
To Spenthrift Sons eternal Fathers gives,
And Health untaintable to modern Wives ;
The Maiden's pious Vows are ftill repaid
With Hufbands bad at Board, and worfe abed ;

H   To

To *Britain* (every Plume of Glory won)   25

Sends News-papers, and all the Work's undone:

Or, juft as Party thinks to crown her Pains,

Gives Refolution, and the Prince ftill reigns.

Before his Feet was plac'd, Slave of his Sway,

NECESSITY whom Men and Gods obey,   30

Her ftrong Right-hand a pond'rous Hammer held,

Her left with Adamantine Nails was fill'd,

Clofe to her Side, of Steel an Anvil rofe,

(The founding Anvil never feels Repofe)

With thefe on this, as faft as FATE affents,   35

She rivets Actions down to their Events.

Millions of *Second-caufes* claim in vain

Their Seat ufurp'd, and urge their Right to reign;

She holds Poffeffion ftill; while they purfue,

For ever, their rejected Suit anew.   40

On

On ev'ry Side, and fcatter'd ev'ry Way,

Her finifh'd Labours in wild Parcels lay

Unrang'd by their Importance, equal here

The Lofs of Battles, or at Whift appear ;

A Statefman chang'd, or Lodging newly lett,   45

Empires transferr'd, or Fafhions out of Date.

The Joys, the Woes, th' Extinction of Man's Race

Serve but to make the Litter of the Place.

Here, trebly clench'd the dire Injunction lay

For War t' extend his yet too narrow Sway ;   50

Hunger or Luft the Conteft firft began,

Ambition foon improv'd upon the Plan ;

Religion next inflam'd the fell Debate,

And fteel'd our Hearts, and edg'd our Swords with Hate ;

Laft, Commerce for an endlefs Quarrel ftood,   55

And all before feem'd Penury of Blood.

There, was ordain'd, Law fhould untie her Noofe,
And flip the Dogs of Licence and Abufe;
To their own Kennels' Stench familiar grown,
But pois'ning ev'ry Nofe except their own;   60
They with full Cry the dubious Scent explore,
And trail wherever Scandal touch'd before:
Still, oh the Shame! ftill the loud Yelp proceeds,
And the firft Head of all the Foreft bleeds.

Here, in like Volume, the Decree of FATE   65
Forbids that Madmen fhould divide the State;
They with abfurd, illib'ral, defp'rate Pufh,
To fhame ev'n Party, and make Faction blufh,
Strive, but in vain, to alienate the Hearts
Of a whole People great in Arms and Arts;   70
To us, by Nature, Reafon, Int'reft, Blood,
Conjoin'd; and union'd by the circling Flood.

I   Thro'

Thro' thefe as FOLLY pafs'd with tott'ring Gait,

From thinking Hurry gave an Air of State,

And tripping at the laft unlucky Law,   75

(As Witches ftumble o'er a Crofs of Straw)

She chanc'd to kick one Bundle, light it roll'd

Into Exiftence; in it was foretold.

A *Mock-heroic* fhould employ the Pains

Of venal Quills, and Party-heated Brains.   80

She, on her Knees, with Hands devoutly clos'd,

At once her Meffage and herfelf, expos'd;

To whom in anfwer FATE: " Thus far to come,

" Swell all its Rage, and lafh itfelf to foam,

" O'er ev'ry Mound of Decency to ride,   85

" Has been allow'd to Riot's Moon-drawn Tide;

" Here its proud Waves fhall ftop, the boift'rous Flood

" On which ye hull'd defert you in the Mud.

"·The

" The Mifts that veil the Morning of this Reign,

" The Breath of Order fhall difperfe again,   90

" Broke they fhall fcud before the piercing Ray,

" And add new Glories to its Burft of Day.

" See the glad Profpect fhine ! a Briton born,

" Whom Virtues, more than you could wifh, adorn,

" Gives Luftre to the Throne; whofe Deeds confefs 95

" No Thirft of Pow'r, except the Pow'r to blefs;

" Who from the Sceptre no Exemption draws,

" And is but the firft Subject of the Laws;

" Ev'n *Monarch* reckons in his moral Plan,

" But fecond Title to the HONEST MAN.

" Him, did the World deferve, Heav'n had defign'd

" The Sov'reign, as the Friend of all Mankind,

" Plac'd

" Plac'd as it's gentle Delegate he'd ftood,

" And won them by Example to be good;

" Taught them the focial Duties how to blend,   105

" The Son, the Brother, Hufband, Father, Friend.---

" Rouz'd from their Dream, the Honeft and the Wife.

" Shall view Confufion with abhorrent Eyes;

" Nay, the mifled fhall fay, while drops the Tear,

" How could our Love be fcribbled into Fear?"   110

" Go, tell your Senders to revere their K--g.---

" And in your private Ear, this only thing

" Of which it can be capable, receive;

" 𝕱𝖔𝖑𝖐𝖘 𝖔𝖋 𝖞𝖔𝖚𝖗 𝕬𝖌𝖊 𝖍𝖆𝖇𝖊 𝖓𝖊𝖇𝖊𝖗 𝖑𝖔𝖓𝖌 𝖙𝖔 𝖑𝖎𝖇𝖊."

Nor more :--- And FOLLY backward on her Way 115

Sullen and filent turn'd her Steps, tow'rds Day.

Andi

And, oh fair Decency! to whom we owe

That Peace and Order are Things known below,

That Man was taught, with better Aim, to pufh

Beyond his Acorn Feaft and Bed of Rufh,   120

The rugged Cavern's Shelter to difown,

And feek Convenience in the peopled Town,

There to diftinguifh, in Subjection mild,

'Tween reafonably free and ftaring wild;

Do thou forgive, if ftung with honeft Pain,   125

Too far o'er Satire's far too open Plain

I urge the fportive Steed, while I purfue

Through his own Paths, the blatant Beaft in view.---

Do thou forgive, if e'er I, unexact,

Of his own Dirt fome little Specks contract;   130

Hard were the Tafk to thrid fo foul a Way,

And yet no plafhing of the Soil betray.

But

But if provok'd to vindicate thy Laws,

I dip my Pen in Truth and Virtue's Caufe,

If I, when Scandal fhoots her Load of Shame, 135

Reftore it honeftly to whence it came;

If my fole Aim is Licence to reftrain,

And laugh thy Rebels home to thee again;

If, undefirous of the Wreath of Bays,

Nor over ticklifh to the Straw of Praife, --- 140

Unafk'd, unpromis'd, if thefe Lines I pour,

Conviction-drawn, but from my Soul abhor

The Name of Satirift, who to his Share

Needs but an Ear to rhime, and Front to dare,

To hide his fplendid Bile in moral Mafk, 145

And fet himfelf at once about his Tafk;---

As a rough Water-Dog, New-England's Breed,

Frefh plaifter'd from fome Pond with Mud and Weed,

I

Round

Round from his Fleece the dirty Puddle shakes

Rejoicing in the Spatter that he makes :---

If These my Motives, not alone forgive,

But bid this JUST RETALIATION, live ;

While Libels, when they've flourish'd for a spirt,

Fall like their Brother Leaves, and rot to Dirt.

F I N I S.

www.ingramcontent.com/pod-product-compliance
Lightning Source LLC
Chambersburg PA
CBHW031244260626
47169CB00007B/2443